Hi Everyone

I've been so busy with all my horses this year that I haven't had a lot of time for writing. But I'm delighted to be back with four brand new stories about Tilly and her beloved horse, Magic Spirit. My new stories will all focus on Tilly and Magic's partnership as they work together and compete at a higher level. Tilly's way of riding reflects my own way of riding. The advice that Tilly is given is what I would teach from my past experiences, and it's also how I've been taught. Over my career it's what I have found has worked for me as I've competed with my horses, so I hope you find it useful, but most of all I hope you will enjoy reading Tilly and Magic's new adventures as much as I have enjoyed writing them.

Keep reading, keep riding and follow your dreams!

See you soon.

Tilly's Horse, Magic

Team Spirit
Team Training
Team Work
Team Magic (coming soon)

Tilly's Pony Tails

Magic Spirit
Red Admiral
Rosie
Samson
Lucky Chance
Solo
Pride and Joy
Neptune
Parkview Pickle
Nimrod
Moonshadow
Autumn Glory
Goliath
Buttons
Rusty
Royal Flame
Stripy
Free Spirit

Pippa Funnell

Orion
Children's Books

First published in Great Britain in 2015
by Orion Children's Books
an imprint of the Hachette Children's Group
and published by Hodder and Stoughton Limited
Orion House
5 Upper St Martin's Lane
London WC2H 9EA
An Hachette UK Company

1 3 5 7 9 8 6 4 2

The paper used in this paperback by Hachette Children's Group
is a natural recyclable product made from wood grown in sustainable
forests. The manufacturing processes conform to the environmental
regulations of the country of origin.

A catalogue record for this book is
available from the British Library.

ISBN 978 1 4440 1202 6

Printed and bound by
CPI Group (UK) Ltd, Croydon, CR0 4YY

www.orionchildrensbooks.co.uk

To all my dedicated
head girls over the years

One

The sun was setting over the tree tops behind the barn at Hancocks Event Yard. Specks of hay dust twirled in the dusky light. As Tilly made her final round of checks, making sure every horse was clean, fed and comfortable, she smiled to herself. She couldn't believe she'd spent most of the holidays working for top international event rider, Livvy James.

Tilly had managed to impress Livvy during a British Junior Squad training week, which had been held at Hancocks. In turn, Livvy had asked Tilly to help in the yard over the holidays.

Luckily, Livvy and Angela, Silver Shoe Farm's owner, were old friends, so Angela had agreed, even though she was losing one of her star stable hands for a week. And even though Tilly was busy at Hancocks, she still visited Silver Shoe every day. She'd learned to ride there and it had also become the home of her very special horse, Magic Spirit.

Magic needed his daily exercise, not to mention feeding, grooming and mucking out. Everyone at Silver Shoe knew these tasks were best left to Tilly, as Magic could frequently be a real handful, but never when Tilly was looking after him. Their bond was extraordinary.

It was hard work, committing time to two yards, but the crazy long hours – up at five in the morning, home at seven in the evening – were worth it. This way, Tilly was getting to learn the ropes in one of the busiest event yards in the country and *still* being there for her favourite horse.

Today was even busier than usual. In addition to her duties at the yards, she was having a rare evening out. Anna, her Junior Squad team mate and bass guitar fanatic, was playing a gig with her band at the local rugby club. Tilly couldn't wait to hear Anna's music, but more importantly, she couldn't wait to see another of her team mates, Harry Grey, who was also going to be there. Aside from being an excellent rider, Harry just happened to be gorgeous, funny and kind.

Tilly brushed the hay out of her hair, checked her watch and walked across the yard. She had less than an hour to exercise Magic, before she had to hurry home, shower, choose an outfit, put some make-up on (something she rarely did), and get to the rugby club in time for the opening song. She searched for her phone. It wasn't in her breeches or the front pocket of her hoody. Suddenly, she noticed Livvy James striding towards her with the phone in her hand.

'Looking for this?'

'Oh, yes,' said Tilly, remembering that she'd been texting her great friend, Mia, during her break. 'Thanks. I was starting to panic. I need to call my dad for a lift.'

'Are you going to Silver Shoe?'

Tilly nodded.

'I'll take you,' said Livvy. 'I'm heading that way anyway. And *actually* there's something I want to discuss with you.'

'Oh,' said Tilly, intrigued. 'Okay, thanks.'

It wasn't until they were in the car – a magnificent 4x4, a prize from one of Livvy's many event wins – that Livvy started to explain.

'I know you're incredibly busy, Tilly,' she said. 'And that you'll have to go back to normal Silver Shoe hours once school starts again in September, but there is one more favour I'd like to ask you.'

Tilly looked up. She'd do anything for Livvy. Having one of her all-time event heroines take an interest in her riding career was a dream come true.

'I'm taking Seasonal Jester to Germany next week. It's Lühmuhlen, one of my favourite four star competitions.'

Tilly nodded. She knew Seasonal Jester. She'd tacked him up a few times and had watched Livvy training him in the massive sand school. He was a fine chestnut thoroughbred with great paces and plenty of scope for jumping, but very sensitive.

'But sadly,' Livvy continued, 'Andrew, my usual groom, has to fly back to Ireland for a funeral. I need a replacement. Someone who's reliable, someone who's passionate, someone who'll do the very best job they can . . .'

Tilly guessed what Livvy was going to say next. Her stomach fluttered with butterflies.

'Would you be able to step in, Tilly? All expenses paid. You'd have to sleep in the horsebox, but there's plenty of room. It's a great competition and you'll learn an awful lot. Only thing is, you'll need a passport.'

'I've got a passport,' said Tilly, stumbling to get the words out quickly enough.

'So, that's a yes?'

'Triple yes!'

'Excellent. I had a few other people in mind, but *you* are the one I wanted most. I think you're ready for some experience on the international circuit. Although, before we get carried away, we'd better check with your parents.'

'They'll say yes,' said Tilly confidently, already calling home.

She knew her mum and dad would be delighted by the opportunity. They, of all people, understood exactly what it would mean to her.

Twenty minutes later, having got the *yes* she wanted, Tilly was in the yard at Silver Shoe, tacking up Magic. She made sure his noseband was sitting comfortably and gave him a pat.

'Lühmuhlen, Magic! Can you *believe* it? *Lühmuhlen!* I'm going to groom for Livvy James!'

Magic gave a snicker and swiped the early evening gnats with his tail.

'Only thing is,' Tilly continued, her voice dropping to a whisper. 'It'll mean leaving you.'

Suddenly, a knot of stress replaced the happy flutter. Magic responded by prodding Tilly's cheek with his nose, bothering her for a cuddle. She ran her hands across his silky coat and snuggled into him. Leaving Magic for any length of time was always difficult. She'd had to do it before, for holidays and school trips, and she'd missed him terribly. But *now*, now there was another reason why leaving was going to be hard.

Tilly and Magic had been close ever since Tilly had helped rescue him from a busy roadside. Their bond had been instant and it had grown and grown, but the fact remained, Magic was an abandoned horse that had been rescued. He wasn't officially Tilly's. Recently, a man called Fred Webb had started emailing her. He'd read about Magic's eventing success in the local papers and was now claiming to be

Magic's rightful owner – and he wasn't being particularly friendly about it.

As Tilly walked Magic out of the yard, the thought of Fred Webb's claims made her feel sick with anxiety. She wished he'd just go away. She hadn't replied to any of his emails and she hadn't talked to her parents or Angela about them. Somehow talking out loud would make them seem even more real and she wasn't ready for that. She was scared her mum and dad might say it was the law and that she'd be forced to give Magic up. The only person she had confided in was her half-brother, Brook, and they'd both agreed to keep quiet, in the hope that the problem would simply disappear. Either way, the idea of leaving Magic alone for any time at all was worrying. What if Fred Webb sneaked into Silver Shoe and took him?

Brook would help though, Tilly thought. He'd be able to keep an eye on things.

Tilly cantered Magic across the field, allowing him to have a playful buck as he lengthened his stride, then headed for one of her favourite paths back to Silver Shoe. As she turned through the gate, she glanced at her watch. Nearly seven. She'd been enjoying the ride so much, time had flown. Now she was running late! She got back to the yard as quickly as she could, removed Magic's tack, offered him some water and gave him his feed, settled him for the night, then called her dad for a lift.

When she was finally home, Tilly did her best to forget her worries about Fred Webb and focused on getting ready for her night out. After lots of deliberation, she chose a pair of cut-off skinnies, neon flip-flops, a short-sleeved Fred Perry blouse, and a long horseshoe pendant. She took her hair out of its plaits, ruffled the waves, practised her kissing face in the mirror, then added a slick of lip-gloss. She took one last look and hardly recognised herself, but she thought she looked okay. As she said goodbye to her parents and made for the front door, her younger brother, Adam, raised his eyebrows.

'Who are *you* trying to impress?'

'None of your business,' she retorted.

He just laughed, as if he knew better.

On the corner of her road, Tilly met her team mates, Ben and Kya.

'Hi,' she said. 'Thanks for waiting for me.'

'No probs,' said Ben. 'We're honoured you've managed to join us. We know you've been a busy bee. How's it going at Livvy's?'

Tilly grinned. She had so much to tell him, especially about her latest invitation to groom at Lühmuhlen. Before she had the chance to speak, however, Kya shot her an envious glare.

'Obviously you're not the only one who's been busy,' she said. 'I've been competing Bastion all over the country. In fact, it's been our most successful month yet. We've won rosettes every time out.'

Despite being team mates, Tilly and Kya didn't get on. They were polite most of the time, for the sake of everyone else in the Junior Squad, but under the surface, their rivalry bubbled. Kya had made mean comments about Magic being 'stolen' and she seemed determined to turn everything between them into a competition, from the pedigree of their horses, to their riding skills, to boys.

Not surprisingly, this evening, Kya was perfectly made-up and wearing a glitzy sequined top and gorgeous designer jeans. She flicked her ice-blonde hair, looked Tilly up and down, then gave a sneery sort of smile.

'Nice to see you wearing something *other* than those dreary beige breeches,' she said.

It was obvious she was referring to Tilly's lucky pair, which – *okay* – she did wear rather a lot (because they were so comfortable to ride in). But why did Kya have to make a point about it?

'I *like* those breeches,' she replied, determined not to get annoyed by Kya's cattiness. 'But they're in the wash. I need them for next Monday.'

'What's happening on Monday exactly?' asked Ben.

'Um . . .' said Tilly hesitantly, not really

wanting to give away her exciting news in front of Kya. 'Livvy's asked me to groom at Lühmuhlen for her. Her usual groom had to drop out.'

Kya fell silent.

'Wow!' said Ben. 'Tilly, that's brilliant!'

Kya frowned.

'Must have been desperate,' she whispered, just loud enough for Tilly to hear.

As they approached the rugby club, they could hear Anna's band doing their sound-check. They walked in, bought their tickets, and found a place to stand near the stage. Anna saw them and waved.

'How cool does *she* look!' said Tilly, waving back.

'Too cool for school,' said a familiar voice behind her.

It was Harry Grey.

'Oh, hi!'

'Hey, you look nice.'

'Thanks,' said Tilly, blushing.

The amps were so loud that, in order to be

heard, Harry had to stand extra close. As he leaned in, Tilly could feel herself going redder and redder.

'I bet there aren't that many riders who have blue Mohawks and play bass guitar!' he shouted. 'Do you want a drink? I'm buying.'

'Um, sure,' said Tilly. 'I'll have a coke. I need the caffeine to keep me awake!'

'Let's go to the bar. By the way, I was wondering . . . do you fancy going out for a ride with me? I wondered about next Monday?'

Tilly blinked.

'Hacking?'

'Yeah, hacking. You know, that thing we seem to spend our whole lives doing.'

'Just you and me?'

'And Magic. And Hunter. Otherwise it would be more of a walk than a hack!'

Tilly laughed.

'I see what you mean,' she said, beaming. 'I'd really like to but . . . I'm afraid I'll be on my way to Germany.'

'Germany?'

'I'm grooming for Livvy at Lühmuhlen.'

'*Nice!* Oh well, maybe another time?'

'Yeah. Sure. Another time.'

As the music started, Tilly tensed. How unfair was *that*? Why did two majorly good things have to clash? Her only hope was that Harry would still be interested enough to ask her out again, after her trip.

Two

The week between Anna's gig and leaving for Lühmuhlen flew by. There was a lot to organise, so much equipment and competition gear. Livvy made several checklists for Tilly so that nothing would be forgotten. In between duties at Silver Shoe and looking after Magic, there was barely time for Tilly to get excited. And then it was Monday evening, the day of departure.

Tilly kissed her dad goodbye and thanked him for dropping her off at Livvy's so late in the evening. Livvy liked to drive through the night, it meant less queuing for the ferry in Dover and a lot less traffic around. If the journey went to plan they would arrive in Lühmuhlen late on Tuesday afternoon.

Tilly gasped when she saw all the lights on in Livvy's amazing horse box. It was parked next to the main stable block, its engine humming quietly.

'Hi there, Tilly, we're all ready, just got to load the horses,' said Livvy as she climbed down the steps, having put her last bit of luggage in the living area of the lorry.

'Horses?' Tilly enquired, feeling puzzled.

'Yes, we're taking Greg Watson's horse, Skydiver,' Livvy explained.

'Greg Watson? The Greg Watson from Australia?' Tilly couldn't believe what she was hearing.

'And the great Skydiver?' She could hardly contain her excitement. 'As in, who won the world championships last year?'

'Yes, that's them,' Livvy replied in a very matter of fact manner. 'Greg is meeting us there, he's flying out to Germany.'

Livvy explained that Greg's original lift to Lühmuhlen had fallen through, because their horse had gone lame, so she'd offered him a lift. It halved travel expenses for both of them, which was an added bonus.

Tilly could hardly believe this was happening to her; she was going to spend a week at Lühmuhlen with two of her absolute idols.

'G'day, I'm Sally, Greg's groom,' said a tall, rather skinny blonde girl, wearing a green and yellow team Australia sweatshirt.

Tilly introduced herself and the girls chatted away as they put the travelling gear onto the horses.

Both horses leapt up the ramp into the horse box keenly, not knowing the length of the journey ahead of them.

Sally decided she wanted to sleep, so went into the living area of the horse box while Tilly climbed up into the passenger's seat. The cab's interior was immaculate. Tilly knew already that Livvy liked everything neat and orderly. Her vehicles were no exception.

'We're going to be sitting in here for nearly twenty hours,' Livvy said. 'So cleanliness counts!'

Tilly agreed. Aside from being the tidiest, it was also the most luxurious horse box she'd ever travelled in. The cab had everything: iPod dock, mini TV, satnav, drinks holders and fully reclining seats. She adjusted the pillow she'd bought from home and popped another mint in her mouth. It was nearly midnight, so the motorway was quiet. They were on their way to the ferry terminal, with Seasonal Jester and Skydiver safely in the back and a non-stop drive through Europe ahead of them.

'Choose whatever music you want,' said Livvy, handing Tilly her iPod.

Tilly scrolled through. She selected an old Queen album that her dad loved. Livvy nodded.

'Good choice. It's appropriate listening to *Under Pressure* in the build-up to a competition. Hopefully, we'll be playing *We Are the Champions* on the way home.'

They both began singing along. Then after a

period of quiet, Tilly couldn't resist asking, 'Do you think Jester has a chance?'

Livvy sighed.

'Honestly, Tilly, I don't know.'

Tilly noticed she gripped the steering wheel more tightly, as though the thought of winning, or not winning really bothered her.

'He's done well so far, hasn't he?' she said encouragingly.

'He has. But Lühmuhlen is new for him. It attracts the best riders and horses from all over the world. I believe he's got what it takes to keep up with them, but who knows . . .'

'At least you've had the experience of competing there before, with other horses. You'll show him what to do.'

'Yes, but every new course with a different horse has new challenges.'

Tilly started to wonder. Something about the competition was obviously bothering Livvy, but she was keeping it to herself. Tilly had always admired how determined she was. She took things very seriously, from running the yard, to her own fortunes in competition. Maybe that's why she and Tilly got on so well. Determination was a trait Tilly recognised in herself – and also in her brother, Brook, another talented rider. Thinking of Brook, Tilly decided to call him, even though it was so late.

'Hello?'

'Hi. It's Tilly.'

'Hey, sis! You must be on your way?' said Brook sleepily.

'We are,' she said, flashing a side-ways smile at Livvy. 'We have a ferry at 2.00 am. And guess who else we have on the lorry? Skydiver!'

'You're kidding? How cool is that?' he said.

'I wish I was joining you. I'd love to go to Lühmuhlen and to meet Greg. I'm seriously jealous.'

'In a few years, you will,' said Tilly. 'You'll be competing.'

'Hope so,' said Brook. 'At the moment, Solo and I have got our eye on the junior championships. But if we do well in those, then it's time to start planning our next steps.'

'You'll win the championships,' said Tilly, grinning.

'Well, we certainly stand a chance. Solo's fit. I'm fit. All being well, I think we've got a chance of pulling it off!'

'*Yeah*!'

They both laughed.

Then Brook whispered, 'And don't worry, Tilly. I'll visit Silver Shoe every day. I'll keep watch over Magic Spirit while you're gone. Trust me, everything will be fine. You just enjoy yourself and make sure Seasonal Jester looks his best!'

'Thanks. Got to go now, big bro. We're just coming into Dover.'

Livvy carefully drove the horsebox onto the weighbridge and collected a ticket with the weight of the lorry and its contents, horses and all, printed on it. Then she pulled up at one of the many kiosks signposted 'Freight Only', while cars were directed to a different area.

Livvy handed in all the passports, both human and equine, along with the export licenses and all the other paperwork connected with travelling horses abroad.

'Nice calm crossing tonight, girls,' said the friendly inspector checking their passports.

On seeing the name on Livvy's passport, he explained that his daughter was one of her biggest fans, and asked for her autograph.

Finally, they embarked with hazard lights flashing, warning that they had special cargo on board. They parked and dropped the ramp of the lorry.

'It can get quite stuffy down here in the hold, so the more air that circulates the better it is for the horses,' Livvy told Tilly.

'If you help Sally offer the horses some water and then give them a haynet each, that will keep them occupied during the crossing.'

Tilly responded quickly while Sally took the horses' top rugs off.

'It can get really warm down here too,' she said.

The three of them left Jester and Skydiver happily munching away, and made their way up to the deck with the duty free shop, so they could stock up with magazines and chocolate.

'Will the horses be ok left all alone,' enquired Tilly, concerned.

Livvy said that they would be. They were used to travelling, and ship's rules stated that no passengers were allowed in the hold.

'They do have someone who walks round and checks, and if they're worried about anything then they'll send someone to escort us down, which is what happens on the longer ferry trips, but as this is only an hour and forty-five minutes the horses will be fine.'

Once the ship had finally docked in the port of Calais, Tilly and Sally replaced the horses' rugs. Skydiver sloshed water over Tilly playfully as he drank, while Jester flatly refused to even get his nose wet.

'We'll stop in a couple of hours' time to offer them more water,' said Livvy, sounding slightly concerned.

It was only then that Tilly realised how important it was not to let the horses dehydrate when travelling.

Two hours later having crossed the French-Belgium border, they found a large area to park, away from the main AutoRoute. They unloaded the horses and gave them a good walk to stretch their legs and allow them to pick at some grass.

Livvy walked over with a bucket of water and placed it on the ground next to Jester.

'Come on boy,' she said, patting him fondly.

To her relief he put his nose deep into the water and had a long drink.

Contented, he turned and nuzzled at Livvy's pocket. Knowing exactly what he wanted, Livvy pulled out a packet of mints. Their affection for one another was obvious. It made Tilly think of her close bond with Magic Spirit. She hoped he was okay. She was glad that Brook would be keeping a close eye on him.

'We should get back on the road,' said Livvy, after a while. 'We'll pick up something to eat when we stop for fuel.'

'Okay,' said Tilly, suddenly feeling hungry.

They set off down the motorway. To Tilly, it felt strange to be driving on the other side of the road, but clearly Livvy wasn't troubled by it.

'I'm used to it,' she said. 'I've competed in Europe many times and I've always driven.'

Tilly loved trying to read the signs. Livvy kept correcting her accent.

'Do you speak fluent French?' asked Tilly, impressed.

'Not fluent,' said Livvy, 'but enough to get by. And a bit of German and a bit of Italian. You?'

'I'm learning at school,' said Tilly. 'But to be honest, I'm not that good. I'd rather be riding.'

'Fair enough,' said Livvy, 'but my advice is to make the most of your education. Through running my yard and competing all over the world, I've discovered that having maths, language skills, and a bit of science is invaluable.'

'Tell me more about your competitions,' said Tilly eagerly. 'What was your favourite ever win?'

'Hmm, I guess it would have to be Kentucky,

riding my old, faithful Evening Star. That was the competition that really got me noticed. I've been fortunate and I have some fantastic memories, but I've also had competitions that have gone very wrong.'

Tilly blinked.

'Lühmuhlen?'

Livvy fixed her gaze on the road ahead.

'Let's just say that the last time I competed at Lühmuhlen, I lost out and it really hurt my pride. I thought I should have won, but in the end . . . look, there's a petrol station. Let's pull over.'

It was obvious she didn't want to say any more and Tilly didn't want to push her by probing. They pulled into the forecourt. Livvy handed Tilly and Sally a bundle of euros and told them to go in and buy some food for the rest of the drive. Inside the shop, they were overwhelmed by all the biscuits, crisps, drinks and confectionery. Not sure what Livvy would like, they bought a selection. They returned to the lorry with their arms full, just as Livvy finished filling the fuel tank. When she saw the huge hoard of treats, she raised an eyebrow.

'I was thinking more along the lines of fruit, nuts, cereal bars and water. Food to give us nutrition and hydration . . . not all this . . . this *junk food*.'

Tilly's face fell. She wanted to be the best competition groom Livvy had ever had. Bad start.

'I – I can go in and exchange it all,' she said.

Livvy softened.

'Don't worry,' she said, breaking into a smile. 'I think we'll survive on . . . *ketchup crisps!* Goodness knows what there'll do to our insides and I certainly wouldn't feed them to any of my horses, but hey . . . you only live once.'

Tilly smiled too, relieved.

'I *am* human, you know,' said Livvy, giving Tilly a nudge. 'I know I can be pretty steely when it comes to competition, but you don't need to be wary of me. I chose you, Tilly. I believe in you. Come on. How about some more Queen to see us through Belgium.'

Tilly jumped into the cab, feeling happy and excited and nervous all at the same time.

'Lühmuhlen here we come!'

Three

After travelling through the night and day and having taken it in turns to make Livvy tea and coffee and regularly checking the horses, Tilly woke from a doze to see a road sign saying: Fur Lühmuhlen Gehen Sie Gerade Aus.

'That means straight on,' said Livvy. 'We're not far now.'

Tilly yawned. Her mouth was dry and her eyes were puffy. Still, she'd had more rest than Livvy, who'd been driving the whole time. Livvy didn't complain though.

'Only a couple of kilometres to go now,' she said.

Tilly shivered with excitement. She couldn't wait, but she knew she wasn't just there for fun. There was work to be done. The inspection and trot up started tomorrow, with dressage on Thursday or, depending on the drawn order, Friday, followed by cross country on Saturday and show jumping on Sunday. Seasonal Jester had to be groomed, plaited, tacked, exercised, sponged, hosed, fed and watered throughout the week – and to the best of Tilly's ability. She was going to be busy.

They pulled off the road and onto a farm track which ran alongside part of the cross country course. At the foot of a hill, fronted by a lake and surrounded by trees, the event stables came into view. It was so pretty. Livvy parked the lorry. Tilly jumped out and took a photo on her phone, which she sent to Brook, Harry, Ben, Anna, and even Kya.

So this is home for the next five days. T xxx

There were several other lorries already lined up in neat rows. Tilly checked the number plates to see where they'd come from: Austria,

Italy, the Czech Republic, the Netherlands, and the biggest one of all, a flashy six-horse navy and gold horsebox from Spain.

A rather plump woman came out of the stable manager's office. When she saw Livvy, she threw her arms in the air.

'Guten Tag! Mein Liebling, Livvy! Wie geht's?'

She pulled Livvy into a hug. Livvy kissed her on both cheeks, then turned to Tilly.

'Tilly, meet Ute Hildegard. She's the stable manager. And she's a dear friend.'

'Hallo,' said Ute, now pulling Tilly into a squeezy hug.

Tilly smiled.

'Hi,' she said.

'It's so busy this year,' Ute explained, with a thick German accent. 'We have riders from all over the world.'

She took Tilly and Livvy by the arm and led them through the temporary stabling. As they got to their stables, her voice dropped to a whisper.

'And I'm afraid, Livvy, I have to admit, you are stabled opposite your not-so-good friend . . .'

'So, that's *his* enormous lorry blocking one of the alleyways?' said Livvy, pulling a face.

'I have no say in who enters this competition,' Ute shrugged.

'As long as he stays out of my way,' Livvy grumbled.

Tilly and Sally unloaded the horses and took all of their boots off, gave them another drink then led them to the large area of grass at the far end of the stable field.

Despite their long journey, both horses were too interested in all the goings-on to eat grass, so it was actually quite the opposite. Rather than Tilly taking Jester for a walk, he marched off, half dragging Tilly behind him, with his new best friend Skydiver hotly in pursuit, and Sally bringing up the rear.

Meanwhile, Livvy went to the event organisers to collect her competition numbers, passes and meal tickets, as well as passes for Lord and Lady Pankhurst, the loyal owners of Seasonal Jester, who were coming to see Livvy and Jester in action.

Jester's stable was at the end of a long, wide temporary stable block. The stall itself was ample. Tilly opened four bags of shavings, spread them around and fetched fresh water. As she worked, she listened to the chatter in the aisle. She could hear lots of different languages and the occasional word in English. When she heard a horse whinny as it walked past, she couldn't resist bobbing her head out to see who'd arrived.

An elegant bay gelding was being led into a stall. He had amazing muscle tone and from the way he moved, Tilly could tell he would be light on his feet. Behind him, a second horse entered – another thoroughbred with a beautiful face. Tilly tingled all over, thrilled to be surrounded by such amazing horses.

A little while later, as she was hanging up a haynet, she noticed the busy chatter drop. Again, she looked out to see what was happening. The grooms in the aisle parted. People started to whisper as a majestic smoke-black stallion entered, and was led into the stable opposite Seasonal Jester's. Tilly recognised the stallion immediately: Midnight Majesty. She'd seen him on TV, competing at Badminton and Burghley, ridden by the well known Spanish three-day eventer, the king of Spain's son, Salvatore Alvarez. They were one of the most famous horse and rider combinations on the circuit and always got lots of attention from the press, only because of who he was, nothing to do with his ability.

As Midnight Majesty was led into his stable, Tilly couldn't help but stare. His coat was so rich in colour, it glistened. His face was delicate and his legs and hindquarters were toned and strong. The groom tending him was a young dark- haired man, dressed in a smart navy and gold logo shirt and cream trousers. When he saw Tilly, he nodded.

'Hola,' he said politely.

'Hi,' said Tilly.

A minute later, when the groom wasn't

looking, Tilly got out her phone and took a sneaky selfie with Midnight Majesty in the background. She sent it round her friends with the message:

Look who Jester's neighbour is???!!! T xxx

Immediately, she was bombarded with replies from Ben, Harry, Brook and Anna, who were all delighted she was having a close encounter with such an illustrious horse. Kya, not surprisingly, didn't reply.

For every two horses there was a spare stable to be used as a tack room. Sadly, Sally and Skydiver were in a different block to Tilly and Jester. After settling Jester in Tilly went inside and began unpacking her boxes of equipment. Before they'd left, Tilly had sat down with Livvy and worked out everything that was needed. There was schooling gear, dressage gear, cross country gear and show jumping gear, as well as all the combs, brushes, ointments, grease, hoof oil, hoof picks, spare shoes, tail-wraps, towels, sponges, buckets, and stud kits. In addition, Livvy thought it would be a good idea to carry indelible markers, duct tape, a stopwatch with spare batteries, a fold-up chair and spares of *everything*. Tilly had the feeling she was going to do a lot of carrying during the course of the week!

After a while, the young Spanish groom came in and started sorting out his equipment. He had everything stored in bags and boxes with the same navy and gold logo, which said 'Alvarez' and then listed his sponsors. It looked very grand.

As Tilly filled three large plastic boxes, one for each day of competition, she noticed the Spanish groom was doing the same, but was being meticulously careful about how he packed them. He gave Tilly a smile.

'I like to arrange items in the order in which I'll need to use them,' he explained, in his soft Spanish accent. 'It saves time.'

'Good idea,' said Tilly, rethinking her own

boxes. 'Um, any other tips? I'm new to this. There's so much to think about.'

The groom straightened up.

'Well, I hope you're fit,' he said. 'Three-day events are hard work. Get used to carrying buckets of water. Get used to plaiting. Pay attention to detail. And work out a schedule with your rider, so that every task is done on time. And if your rider is as demanding as mine, you will also need to learn to be a mind reader. Know exactly when he wants to ride, when he wants a drink, and when he wants his stirrups adjusted. Don't wait to be asked. Just *know*.'

'Oh,' said Tilly. 'Thanks. Have you been a groom for a long time?'

'Longer than I dare mention,' said the man. 'I'm Chavez, by the way.'

'I'm Tilly.'

'Nice to meet you, Tilly, new girl. And don't worry – if you follow my advice, you'll do fine.'

Four

The following morning, Tilly's alarm buzzed at 6.30 am. As the warmth of sleep faded, she groaned and forced herself out of bed. She couldn't believe how well she'd slept. She had her own special bed high up in the lobby of Livvy's luxury horse box, accessed by a narrow ladder attached to the wall and cleverly built above the shower and toilet. This lorry had everything; it was like a luxury motor home that just happened to be able to take six horses as well.

Tilly sleepily climbed down the narrow

ladder, trying to be as quiet as she could so she wouldn't wake Livvy.

Livvy was sleeping above the cab in the very spacious living area; it had a kitchen on the left hand side with a large TV centred in the top units and smart navy leather seating surrounding an oak varnished table on the right.

Tilly crept into the horse area to get dressed. The previous day she and Sally had thoroughly mucked and swept out the back, to make room for everyone's clothes, coats and boots.

'Morning, would you like a cup of tea?' came a voice from the living area. Livvy was already up. She was sitting reading last week's *Horse and Hound*.

'Yes please,' replied Tilly popping her head around the door.

She was surprised that Livvy was so wide awake considering she'd missed out on a whole night's sleep.

'Shouldn't you get some more rest after that long drive?' she asked.

'I'd love to but I never sleep that well at the

big competitions, I find it difficult to relax and switch off. Always thinking, 'Have I done this? Have I done that?'

'What can I do to help?' asked Tilly.

'I'm afraid you'll have to stay very switched on,' said Livvy.

'With horses plans can change. I might tell you I'm going to work Jester for forty-five minutes, but if he's fresh and excited, I could be on him for a lot longer. Or I might suddenly want to change his bit.'

Tilly looked concerned.

'Don't worry I don't expect you to mind read.'

'Most importantly always make sure Jester has water and a clean bed, he can be fed at his normal times except on cross country day, but I'll advise you about that.'

'Of course.' Tilly replied.

'This morning I'll take Jester out for a quiet hack and let him take in the sights of the competition venue. We then have the riders' welcome and briefing where we are introduced to the officials. After the briefing the cross country course is open for walking.'

'First walk I always like to do on my own, so that I have no distractions. Your first impressions of fences are very important. If you like, you can walk the course with me on either Thursday or Friday, depending on which day my dressage is.'

'I'd love to,' said Tilly.

'The first vet's inspection is at 3pm, so Jester needs to be plaited and ready for then. The draw will be done after that so we'll wait and find out which day I will be doing dressage to decide what type of work he'll need later.'

Tilly felt relieved that Livvy had informed her of the day's plans.

As they walked through the temporary stable block, they thought they were the first out and about until Tilly noticed Chavez was already mucking out Midnight Majesty.

'Hola, Tilly, new girl,' he called.

Tilly waved and smiled. Livvy, however, marched ahead with pursed lips.

'Word of advice,' she whispered, as Tilly

caught up with her. 'Be careful who you associate with.'

Tilly blinked.

'What do you mean?'

'That's Salvatore Alvarez' groom, isn't it?'

'Yes. He's really nice. He gave me some good tips.'

'I'm sure he did. Just . . . be careful is all I'm saying. Alvarez and his team have a reputation.'

'What kind of reputation?'

'You'll see.'

Tilly was puzzled and began to wonder if Alvarez had anything to do with Livvy's bad experience at Lühmuhlen? She wanted to ask more questions, but she sensed it wasn't the right time.

Livvy jumped down from a rather hot-looking Seasonal Jester.

'Oh boy, have I got my work cut out this week,' she exclaimed.

'Jester is definitely living up to his name, joking around.'

'Is he pleased to be at an important party?' said Tilly, taking the reins from Livvy.

'He's certainly prancing about as if he's at a disco dancing to heavy metal and rap.'

Tilly giggled.

'Let's just hope by dressage day you, young man, are prepared to do some beautiful ballet,' said Livvy, affectionately patting Jester as Tilly led him into his stable to untack.

'G'day young lady, how are you? Long time no see,' said someone, hugging Livvy.

Hearing his strong Australian accent, Tilly peeked through the bars of the stable, as she took Jester's saddle off. It was the first time she'd seen Greg Watson in real life.

'Tilly, I want you to meet a very old friend of mine,' said Livvy, beckoning Tilly.

'Tilly, this is Greg,' she said.

'Greg, this is Tilly, she's helping me out for the week.'

Greg shook Tilly's hand warmly.

'Lucky girl, helping one of the best, if not THE BEST on the circuit.'

Tilly's heart missed a beat. She couldn't quite take it in, that here, right now, she was standing with the two people she had idolised for years.

'Quick, we must dash, we are about to miss the competitor's briefing' said Livvy, suddenly flustered.

'Please can you have Jester ready half an hour before the first vet's inspection,' she called as she hurriedly left the stable block.

Preparations were underway for the vet's inspection, which would give the judges and spectators a chance to preview the horses before the official competition began. It was also an opportunity for the vets to undertake their formal inspection. It was important that Seasonal Jester looked his best in order to make a good impression, but it was also vital that he was fit and sound (not lame) to compete. If he wasn't, Tilly knew he could be eliminated from the competition before it began. Luckily, she'd spent enough time with him to know he was as fit as anything.

She started by shampooing him all over, making sure she washed all the sweat off, then she rinsed and scraped the water off with a sweat-scraper before rubbing him down with a towel. She picked out his hooves, applied hoof oil, and used a detangling spray on his mane and tail. Next she worked his mane, combing, sectioning and plaiting tightly. Her speciality. She worked nimbly, wetting stray hairs to keep everything smooth. When she was done with the mane, she put a tail bandage on his neatly pulled tail. She rubbed a little baby oil around his eyes, nostrils and ears, to keep them clean and moist. For a final trick she put chequered patterns on his quarters to show off his shiny coat.

Having done all this, she couldn't help noticing that Chavez, the Spanish groom, was *still* fiddling with Midnight Majesty's mane –

and he'd started working on it two hours ago! He was struggling to get the plaits as neat and tight as they needed to be. Every now and then, he would mutter crossly and re-do an entire section. Since Tilly found plaiting easy (ever since she was little, she'd had daily practice on her own hair!), she wondered if she should offer to help, but then she thought of what Livvy had said. And anyway, the first few horses were being led out of the stables for the vet's inspection. There was no time to spare.

Moments later, Livvy appeared, dressed in a stylish turquoise jacket and white jeans, ready for the trot up.

'Wow, Tilly,' she said. 'Great job. Jester looks immaculate.'

'Thanks,' said Tilly, feeling proud.

Tilly made sure she had everything she needed in her rucksack for any last minute touch-ups, then grabbed a bottle of water and together she and Livvy walked Jester down to the main arena, where the trot up would be held on a special hard strip of tarmac. Tilly felt very responsible, as though it was all down to her whether Livvy and Jester had a good competition or not. She hoped they were both pleased with her. Maybe there wasn't much glory in being a groom, but it was certainly a job that counted.

Five

Having passed the inspection all sound and well, the competition was now on. The following morning, Tilly's alarm went off early again. Within half an hour, she was washed, dressed and in the stable, ready to groom. As soon as Jester saw her opening the stable door, he pricked his ears and moved forward.

'Good boy,' she whispered, patting his shoulder. 'All set for dressage, then?'

A shaft of light came through a crack in the wooden panels of the wall, signalling the appearance of the sun. It was going to be a beautiful day. Tilly stroked Jester's coat and felt a pang of homesickness, wishing she could transport herself back to Silver Shoe to give Magic Spirit his morning hug. Hopefully Brook would be doing it for her. Meanwhile, she tied Jester up in his stable and then mucked it out. Having done a successful job for the inspection, she now felt more confident about her responsibilities.

Once the stable was clean, it was time to tack Jester up. His dressage was not until later in the afternoon, but as he had been so bright and keen the previous day, Livvy felt she had to work him in the morning.

Tilly took off his summer sheet – it was too warm for any more rugs – folded it and hung it up outside the stable. She gave him a good brush, wiped around his nose and eyes with a damp sponge, then put a set of polo (exercise bandages) on. She carefully placed the numnah and sheepskin pad on his back before putting a dressage saddle on, making sure everything was straight and even.

Just as she was finishing buckling up the noseband, Livvy walked into the stable.

'That's just what I like, punctuality. Thanks,' she said. 'Bang on time.'

Having given Livvy a leg up, and checked the girth, Tilly took the opportunity to grab some breakfast in the groom and riders' canteen at the far end of the stable field.

'Definitely more relaxed today,' said a relieved Livvy, riding back into the stables.

'Sorry, Tilly, I got him rather hot, I think he'll need another bath.'

There was a spacious wash-down area next to the stables. Tilly checked the temperature of the water then began running it down Jester's legs, working her way up to his hind quarters and back. Once his coat was wet, she used a sponge and shampoo to work up a lather. Chavez and Midnight Majesty came to join them.

'Hiya,' said Tilly.

'Hola,' replied Chavez.

Majesty and Jester gave each other a nod as they were bathed next to each other. They both stood patiently, as though they knew exactly what was expected of them. After shampooing, their coats were rinsed and scraped, to remove any excess water, then their faces were sponged and their manes and tails washed and combed.

'You like Lühmuhlen so far?' said Chavez, as he began rubbing Majesty's tail with a towel.

'I love it,' said Tilly.

'The most exciting times are yet to come,' he said. 'Cross country. Show jumping. But we grooms will remain in the background. We're the ones who keep everything going behind the scenes. That's just how it is.'

'Chavez,' said Tilly, curious. 'Do you know if your rider, Alvarez, has any issues with my rider?'

'You mean, Livvy James?'

'That's her.'

Chavez was quiet for a moment. He scratched his head, then ran the hose water over his hands.

'I know that a couple of years ago Livvy and Salvatore were both in contention for first place,' he said. 'And that it didn't end well for Livvy. A shame for her. She's a nice lady and a great rider. But win some, lose some. Salvatore is the son of the king of Spain, he loves to get his own way. No one should expect to beat him.'

Tilly nodded, but something about Chavez' response didn't convince her. Livvy was sensible enough to appreciate that winning and losing were all part of the competition experience, so this didn't explain why she was so wound up by Alvarez. Tilly felt certain there was more to it than simply wanting to beat a successful rival. Before she could say anymore, however, Chavez led Majesty away.

'Plaits,' he muttered. 'Time to get to work on the plaits!'

The event site was a frenzy of activity. There were crowds of spectators, a beer garden, and stalls selling high quality equestrian kit, while the smell of grilled sausages drifted on the warm air. Jester was fascinated by it all and still a little bit excitable so Livvy suggested Tilly lunge him for twenty minutes, to calm him down before she practised the dressage test in the warm-up area. As Tilly lunged Jester round and round, she thought of Chavez' comment about Salvatore Alvarez being the world's number one. He certainly looked the part, with all his expensive branded equipment, but what was it Livvy had said about him having a bad reputation? Maybe he was a bit like Kya – a great rider, with a mean streak.

'That's it Jester,' said Tilly, encouraging the horse along. 'Trot on, steady. Calm as anything. We *really* need you to lead after the dressage for Livvy.'

When it was finally time to get on, Jester was composed. Tilly gave Livvy a leg-up and tightened the girth. Over the next half hour, Tilly watched transfixed as Livvy practised various movements.

'Let's hope I've got the timing correct,' said Livvy, as Tilly removed Jester's exercise boots and gave him one last wipe down.

'Good luck,' she whispered.

She crossed her fingers as she watched them go into the arena down the centre line and salute the judges. Happily, luck wasn't necessary. They sailed through the test. Livvy looked focused and elegant. Jester was supple and relaxed. His flying changes were perfect, as was his trot and canter work, but the thing Tilly was most proud of was the fact that, thanks to her, he looked spectacular. His coat was gleaming.

When the test was complete, Livvy and Jester met Tilly in the collecting ring.

'I'm delighted with him,' said Livvy. 'I always feel better when I know our dressage will put us in a competitive position.'

She gave Jester a hug, then dismounted and waited eagerly for her score to be announced. Tilly had no time to waste. Jester was hot after the test, so she loosened his girth, led him back to the stables and washed him down, sponged his legs, gave him some water and scraped the sweat from his coat. A little while later, Livvy returned with a big smile on her face.

'Lots of nines,' she said, giving a thumbs-up. 'A few eights and a seven, but mostly nines. Just what we needed.'

'Brilliant. How are the other riders doing?'

'The New Zealanders are looking good,' said Livvy. 'And the Germans. And there's a young Italian rider who's making a very promising debut.'

'And the Spanish?' said Tilly cautiously.

'You mean Alvarez?' said Livvy. 'He's done okay. He always does, but we're in the lead after our test.'

Moments later, Alvarez, Chavez and Majesty passed them. It was hard not to notice them, as Alvarez was making lots of fuss, arguing loudly, telling Chavez off and gesturing angrily at a couple of uneven plaits in Majesty's mane. Tilly bristled. It was an uncomfortable sight.

'Oh, no,' she said. 'Looks like poor Chavez is getting the blame for their score.'

‘Typical Alvarez,’ Livvy said, shaking her head. ‘Always so full of himself.’

Later, back in the stable field, Tilly was taking Jester out to graze the lush grass, when she noticed Chavez leading Majesty towards her and looking glum. Even though they were technically rivals, she felt friendly towards him. She hadn’t liked seeing him ridiculed and yelled at, especially in front of spectators and other grooms and riders. Chavez seemed so hardworking and conscientious – and it was obvious that he and Majesty had a close bond. He deserved some respect. Tilly waved him over.

‘Hola,’ she said, trying out her Spanish.

‘Hola, new girl,’ muttered Chavez, without looking up.

‘You okay? If you don’t mind me asking? I saw Alvarez shouting earlier.’

‘Plaits,’ said Chavez. ‘My weakness. I do my

best, but it's never good enough for Alvarez.'

'You know,' said Tilly boldly. 'Maybe you should think about grooming for someone else? Someone who'll *appreciate* you?'

Chavez shook his head.

'But my loyalty is to Majesty. I've known that horse since he was a foal. I've been with him throughout his fabulous career. We come as a pair.'

'Yes, of course,' said Tilly, instantly understanding.

She thought of Magic and how deeply loyal she felt towards him. She remembered how much it had hurt her when Kya had made spiteful comments about his past, implying he'd never be good enough. In Tilly's mind, he was more than good enough. He was everything. She'd stick by him always, no matter what. She twiddled her horsehair bracelets and thought for a moment. An idea came to her.

'I could help you,' she said.

'How?'

'I'll teach you how I plait. I never like to brag,

but when it comes to plaiting . . . it's my thing.'

She held up her own plaits, which she always wore when she was with the horses. Chavez smiled.

'I'll teach you my secret techniques,' she encouraged, 'then Alvarez will have nothing to complain about.'

'New girl, I like your spirit, but I don't think it'll help matters.'

Tilly shrugged and smiled. 'Oh, yeah?'

'We're on rival teams. What would Livvy James say if she knew you were helping me?'

'Maybe our riders are rivals,' said Tilly, 'but we're grooms together. Grooms should support each other. And our horses certainly aren't rivals . . .'

She nodded to Jester and Majesty, who were touching noses as they grazed.

'Okay, okay, Tilly, new girl, you're on. But what's in it for you?'

'Good question,' said Tilly, with a cheeky smile, thinking that she hadn't made a new horsehair bracelet for a while. 'I'd love to have some proof that I've been with Midnight Majesty just so my friends really believe me . . . ?'

That evening, Tilly showed Chavez her techniques for getting even, tight plaits, using a short-toothed pulling comb to divide the mane equally. She demonstrated how she secured each plait with an elastic band, then rolled it into a tight ball, which was sewn in place with a needle and thread. Her thin, nimble fingers made it seem easy, compared to Chavez' chunkier hands. Nonetheless, he enjoyed the lesson.

While he worked on Majesty's mane, Tilly pulled his tail and popped the hairs she collected safely in her pocket. She listened to Chavez sharing some of his grooming stories while they worked. It turned out he'd travelled all over the world to work with Majesty and had given up the idea of having a family or riding horses of his own. His life was all about grooming. Tilly found herself admiring him and feeling sorry for him all at the same time.

'Can you take a photo of me and Majesty, please?' she asked.

She handed Chavez her phone, then leaned forward and smiled as he took the picture, making sure Majesty's handsome face was clearly visible.

'Perfect! Thank you!'

She took her phone back from Chavez. She'd had lots of texts from Harry and the others asking how she was getting on, so she knew they'd be pleased to see this picture. She was about to send it to everyone she could think of, including Kya, who was clearly ignoring her text updates, when she noticed several missed calls and an answer phone message from a unfamiliar number. Tilly thanked Chavez, patted Midnight, then checked the tail hairs safely in her pocket. Perfect. On her way back to the horsebox, she tried to listen to the message. Unfortunately, however, the connection was so poor all she could hear was crackles and hisses.

Not a single word. Nevertheless, after her lovely evening it left an uneasy feeling in her stomach, one that wouldn't go away.

Six

Before Tilly went to sleep that night, she phoned Brook. Maybe it was the mystery phone-call or maybe it was because she was missing Magic. Either way, she felt compelled to call.

'Don't worry. I'll check first thing in the morning,' Brook reassured her. 'You just concentrate on what you've got to do. Are you walking the cross country tomorrow? Actually, on Saturday, Solo and I will be competing ourselves. We've got a one-day event on the outskirts of Cosford. Nothing as glamorous as Lühmuhlen, but apparently there'll be talent spotters there.'

'Sounds great,' said Tilly. 'Show them what you and Solo can do.'

'We will. Anyway, night-night.'

'Good night.'

Feeling much happier, Tilly snuggled up in her duvet and tried to block out her worries by thinking through her tasks for the next day. She was sure Livvy would still be awake too, reliving the applause from the crowds after her excellent dressage.

Having done the dressage on Thursday made Friday a relatively easy day for Tilly. Livvy got Jester ridden in the morning. She took him for a nice long hack with Greg and Skydiver and then gave him a pipe-opener. When Tilly looked puzzled, Livvy explained it was a quick gallop to clear his lungs.

Then just as promised she allowed Tilly to walk the cross country with her.

As they stepped onto the course they could

feel the earth was dry and crumbly.

'If there's no rainfall by tonight, then it's going to be hard underfoot,' said Livvy. 'We'll have to make sure Jester gets plenty of ice on his legs after he's run.'

'Yes,' said Tilly, taking note.

Along the way, Livvy pointed out the various jumps, around twenty-nine in all, over six kilometres. Some of them were nearly 1.30 metres high: brushes, bounces, arrow-heads, tables, ditches, banks, logs, coffins, and tricky combinations. Tilly gulped. She'd always dreamed of taking Magic Spirit to a four star event, but now that the challenge of the cross country course was directly in front of her, the prospect seemed terrifying.

'Stamina, trust, and guts,' said Livvy. 'That's what it takes.'

Tilly nodded.

'Don't freak out,' Livvy continued. 'A four star always looks daunting when you see it for the first time, but if you work hard, prepare well, and believe in yourself, it's achievable.

Now, let's see if we can memorise what we've seen. I like to get a map of the course clear in my mind, then go over and over it, being sure of all the lines I am taking, especially for the large corners and arrowheads. Also, remember where the minute markers are – the place where I have to be at each minute.'

Cross country day was one of the busiest.

The stables were bustling as the first few horses and riders started leaving for their warm up. As Tilly began her grooming routine, she could feel Jester was nearly bursting with energy. He kept bobbing and side-stepping, making it difficult for her to brush him and prepare his studs. He seemed to know the big day had arrived.

Livvy, meanwhile, was very quiet. Tilly watched as she paced up and down the aisle between the stables, in a world of her own, focusing on the challenge ahead. By contrast, Salvatore Alvarez had caused a stir in the stables, surrounding himself with a crowd of journalists and photographers.

'And I also have to thank my fabulous sponsors,' she heard him say, over and over again, as though he'd already won the competition.

He smiled and laughed as if he didn't have a care in the world. At one point, he even called Chavez over for a 'friendly' hug and photo-opportunity. Chavez smiled for the camera, but Tilly could tell from his eyes that he was frowning inside.

When Chavez finally sloped back to his grooming duties, he caught Tilly's attention.

'All about the media,' he whispered. 'Alvarez loves being famous and loves being a prince.'

'But shouldn't he be preparing?' said Tilly. 'He's about to throw himself over a four mile course of solid obstacles. And some of them are enormous!'

She spotted Livvy, quiet and still in a corner of the tackroom, breathing deeply, swigging water, psyching herself up.

'Alvarez doesn't *do* 'preparing', Tilly. He

thinks he's invincible. You know, he hardly pays attention when he walks the cross country.'

'*What*?' said Tilly, shocked.

Having seen those massive jumps and gravity-defying drops, and the way in which Livvy meticulously thought them through, she didn't know whether to be impressed by Chavez's revelation or dismayed. One thing was for certain, she was starting to understand the true depth of Livvy and Alvarez's rivalry. It wasn't just old-fashioned sportsmanship. It was a matter of principle. They stood for different attitudes, for opposite ways of doing things.

Livvy made her way to the cross country warm up area, followed by Tilly pushing a wheelbarrow, with all the equipment she needed. Washing down buckets, sponges, spare shoes, studs, head collar, event grease and a couple of different bits in case of any last minute changes.

Tilly didn't know who was the most nervous, her or Livvy.

Livvy had explained earlier that everybody

suffers from nerves, some more than others, but it was important not to let the nerves affect you. To always try and think positively.

Jester looked spectacular in the warm up, a picture of fitness and health.

Tilly had to avoid his studded hooves as he jigged around impatiently while she tried to apply the grease to his legs. It would help protect him if, for any reason, he hit a fence.

'Four minutes, number 37,' called a tall gaunt-looking German official.

With Jester itching to gallop, Livvy barely responded when Tilly wished her good luck. Tilly wasn't offended. She knew what this moment meant to Livvy, that she was in a 'zone'.

They set off in a good positive rhythm, over the first fence, then up a hill to a wide brush oxer, followed by an arrowhead, then a gaping ditch. They tackled each obstacle with confidence and it was obvious from the speed and efficiency with which they cleared them that Livvy's attention to detail was paying off. Eventually, the course led into the woods and Tilly could no longer see.

She had to rely on the commentators to hear how they were doing. She could hardly breathe she was so tense. It was a great relief when she saw them galloping over the final part of the course. Flying the last to complete a faultless jumping round, with just a handful of costly time faults.

Tilly rushed to greet them. Livvy was like a different person: cheery, relieved and full of joy. As she dismounted, she laughed exuberantly, then threw her arms around Tilly and Jester.

'He did it! He was unbelievable! Amazing!'

'Well done!' said Tilly, stroking Jester's muzzle. 'Well done, boy, you've done us proud!'

'And so have you, Tilly,' said Livvy. 'I'm really glad I chose you to groom for us.'

'I wouldn't have missed it for anything,' replied Tilly as she threw plenty of cold water over a hot, puffing Jester to try and cool him down.

That evening, everyone was in a celebratory mood. The event organisers threw a party for the competitors. Tilly was delighted when Livvy asked her to be her guest.

'We won't stay out late, of course,' Livvy cautioned. 'We need to check that Jester is sound for tomorrow morning's final vet's inspection and we want to be fresh for the show jumping, but I think it's only fair, after all our hard work, we have a bit of fun. It's traditional after the cross country.'

While Tilly was getting ready, she gave Brook a call to find out how he'd done at his one day event. They always called each other after competitions, so that they could give each other commiserations or congratulations (mostly congratulations!).

'How was it?'

'We came first,' said Brook. 'But it wasn't a very strong field.'

Tilly smiled. He was always so modest.

'Sounds like you need a bigger challenge,' she said. 'The small competitions are getting too easy for you!'

'Bring on Lühmuhlen,' he said. 'So you'll be

partying tonight?'

'Sort of,' said Tilly. 'How's Magic?'

'He's good. Missing you, of course, but I trotted him round the sand school a few times and gave him an extra carrot. To be honest, the carrot was the only way I could get him to cooperate for me!'

'That sounds like Magic!'

One of the large marquees next to the main arena had been decorated with ribbons and flowers. There was a live band, a dance floor, and waiters serving delicious drink and food: a hog roast, potatoes, lots of different salads, and a vast display of silky-looking chocolate cakes. Tilly hadn't brought any party clothes, but it didn't matter. Everyone was wearing jeans and t-shirts. She glided around the room looking for famous faces, but couldn't help tuning into the party gossip. The talk of the evening was about how Salvatore Alvarez had messed up on the cross country. Having stated to the press that he was expecting to win, he'd missed his line to a corner, so had a run out, then amidst his fury didn't take time to get re-organized, so had a second refusal. Having not walked the alternative he then nearly got himself eliminated for jumping the wrong course, had it not been for the crowd aiding him in his moment of confusion.

'Serves him right for being such a show-off,' said one rider.

'That man makes my blood run cold,' said another. 'He's so arrogant.'

'I'd find all the celebrity stuff distracting,' said a third. 'Sure, we all benefit from a bit of media exposure, but he takes it too far.'

Notably, Alvarez and Chavez weren't at the party. Tilly ran to find Livvy and tell her the news. She felt bad for Chavez – and for Midnight Majesty – but she knew it would please Livvy, and every rider who took their competition preparation seriously, to hear that their hard work had proved worth it.

Seven

The last day of the competition, the show jumping, came upon Tilly before she'd even had a chance to absorb the excitement of the cross country. Her alarm went off at 5.30am. She had to get Jester ready for the final vet's inspection. Horses had to be passed sound and healthy to jump on the final day.

The sun shone brightly through the skylight in the roof of the lorry. She kicked off her bedclothes and stumbled down the narrow ladder. As she washed and dressed, she could feel aches and pains all over her body. Her legs were stiff from walking everywhere. Her back twinged from carrying tack. And her shoulder was sore from all the extra brushing, washing and polishing of Jester's coat. Chavez was right, grooming at a three-day event required stamina. Tilly didn't mind, of course. The experience was worth it a hundred times over and, although she was looking forward to having a rest and seeing Magic again, she was disappointed it was coming to an end. She downed a large mug of sugary tea, ate two bananas for fuel, then headed out to the stables. Jester was waiting at the door and whickered as soon as he saw her.

'Good morning, mister,' she said, stroking his nose. 'Show jumping later, but let's take those stable bandages off and see how your legs are.'

Jester nibbled her hands and gave a snort. She tickled his ears and rubbed his neck. She'd grown close to him over the last few days and knew she was going to miss him when she got home. She would, however, get to see Magic – which definitely made up for it. As Tilly started forking Jester's bedding, her mind flooded with thoughts of home. She wondered what her friends were up to – Ben, Anna, Harry, Mia, even grouchy Kya, who'd ignored every photo and message she'd sent from Lühmuhlen. She wondered whether Brook and Solo were out riding yet, getting ready for their next one-day event. And, of course, she wondered about Silver Shoe, which would just be coming to life. She pictured Magic's peaceful face and fine grey coat and twiddled her horsehair bracelets, particularly the one made from his tail-hairs. It always made her feel close to him when he wasn't around.

Once the stable was clean, Tilly began her grooming routine. She brushed and polished Jester's coat, then plaited his mane ready for the final vet's inspection. Livvy had trotted Jester up and felt his legs last thing before going to bed, so they were not surprised when he was passed fit to show jump. As it was in reverse order, Livvy was one of the last to jump that afternoon so they all had a long wait. Tilly spent her time packing up the lorry and getting organized for the long journey home with a very tearful Sally. Poor Skydiver had stumbled up the step coming out of the water and had, unbeknown to Greg, over-reached (trodden on the back of his heel). Although he jumped bravely around the rest of the course and was lying in third place overnight, he sadly failed the final inspection. Greg, knowing the sport so well, accepted the rotten luck and was just relieved it was nothing serious.

Livvy came out to the stables dressed in her show jumping gear. She looked fantastic. She looked, thought Tilly, like a winner.

'I'd like to get to the main arena pronto,' she said. 'Jester always needs time to focus before the show jumping.'

'No problem,' said Tilly. 'We're nearly ready.'

'Great,' said Livvy, then she leaned towards Tilly and smiled. 'You know you've really proved yourself in this competition. You've been hard-working, committed and efficient. But most of all, you've given Jester everything he needs. If we get a good result today, it'll be because of your contribution. Eventing is all about team work and I think we've been a great team.'

Tilly grinned.

'Me too,' she said.

Livvy's praise made her feel great. She glanced across the aisle at Chavez and Midnight Majesty. It was such a shame that Salvatore Alvarez couldn't be more encouraging of Chavez' hard work. He deserved better. So did Majesty.

Down at the main arena, while Livvy walked the course and took a few minutes to talk to her owners, Tilly led Jester to a quiet, shaded area where he could get away from the electric atmosphere. Tilly leaned against a tree trunk and admired the sight of him, his magnificent silhouette against a backdrop of blue sky and dramatic German forest. It was such a perfect scene; she decided to take a photo to send to her friends. As she took out her phone, however, she noticed another answer phone message from the mystery phone number. Whoever it was, they were persistent. With a sigh, Tilly pressed play and listened. Again, the line was crackly, but this time she could hear a voice. She turned the volume up, held the phone tight to her ear. A feeling of dread washed over her. Before she heard it all the way through, she *knew*.

'This is a message for Miss Tiger Lily Redbrow,' said a gruff voice. 'My name is Fred Webb and I'm telling you right now, I WANT MY HORSE BACK. I have been *trying* to email you and call you, but you haven't responded, therefore I've decided I'm going to take matters into my own hands. Goodbye.'

His voice sounded grumpy and *very* unfriendly. Hands trembling, heart thumping, Tilly listened to the message again.

I'm going to take matters into my own hands.

She shuddered. What did he mean? Was he going to call the police? Was he going to contact Angela and start questioning her instead? Or worst of all, was he planning to head straight for Silver Shoe to snatch Magic away? And if he snatched him, where would he take him? What would he do with him? Would she ever *see* him again?

Panic took over. Everything went blurry. She gasped and clutched the phone to her chest. Her eyes filled with tears. What could she do? She felt helpless. Suddenly, Lühmuhlen no longer felt like a thrilling adventure. It was torture. Here she was, on the other side of Europe, while Magic Spirit was under threat.

Now that she knew the phone number was Fred Webb's, Tilly wondered if she could call him back. Maybe she could tell him it was all a misunderstanding? Maybe she could explain how much Magic meant to her and make him back off? But the thought of speaking to him made her feel sick. From his tone, he didn't sound like the sort of person who would compromise. No. The only thing she could do was make sure Magic was protected.

She checked her watch. Midday, he'd

probably be out in the field. Maybe even the long field, which was the furthest from the yard, and accessed by a disused track – a track that had once been used by horse thieves in an attempt to steal the Derby winner, Moonshadow, who'd been stabled overnight at Silver Shoe. If it had been used then, it could be used again. Tilly's mind raced.

She thought about calling Angela, but she'd always worried that Angela might feel she had to respect Fred Webb's request. As much as Angela understood Tilly and Magic's bond, she wouldn't want to be accused of keeping a horse unlawfully and she certainly wouldn't want her yard to be given a bad name. Tilly considered calling her parents, but again, she'd been too scared to ask for their advice, assuming they'd agree with Fred Webb.

Brook. The one person she could count on was Brook. He knew. He would understand. She could call him and ask him to go to Silver Shoe and check on Magic himself. Brook could make sure Magic was kept in his stable all day.

There would be too many people and other horses about, for Magic to be stolen from his stable.

Without a second to lose, Tilly tapped in his number. No reply. She tried again, but it went straight through to answer phone.

'Brook! It's Tilly, call me *urgently*, okay?'

She waited with the phone in her hand, willing him to call back straight away. Oblivious, Jester carried on grazing, swishing his tail, and flicking his ears. The longer Tilly waited, the more anxious she got. If Brook was out riding, he could be hours.

Suddenly, Tilly heard her name being called. It was Livvy.

'Time to go! Come on, Tilly! I've been looking *everywhere* for you. We need to get to the warm-up. Are you ready? Is Jester ready?'

Flustered, Tilly grabbed Jester's rein. Because of the drama, she'd lost track of time. She hadn't done any of her last minute grooming tricks, such as applying a fresh slick of hoof oil, and giving his coat a final wipe-down. She hoped

Livvy wouldn't notice, but Livvy was just anxious to warm up and jump some practice fences before going into the main arena to show jump.

'What's going on, Tilly?' she said. 'You look like you're in a daze.'

Tilly opened her mouth to explain, then paused. She decided it wouldn't be fair to offload her problems on Livvy, just as Livvy was about to compete. She remembered how a pre-competition argument with Kya had ruined Kya's performance in the Pony Club Championships. Tilly had felt terrible about it. Even though she and Kya didn't get on, it hadn't been fair to distract her at that moment. And she definitely didn't want to distract Livvy. She blinked, took a deep breath and gathered her inner-strength.

'Everything's fine,' she said. 'I'm just a bit . . . tired.'

'Well, come on, then,' said Livvy. 'Get yourself together.'

Livvy took Jester's reins from Tilly and

marched him ahead. Tilly nodded and followed, desperate not to disappoint the person who'd only just finished telling her what a great team they were.

Eight

As Livvy mounted and began circling in the warm-up arena, Tilly's effort to stay strong collapsed. It was too much. It didn't matter that she was surrounded by eager horses and successful riders, or that the sun was shining, or that the crowds were happy. All she could think about was Magic. She just wanted to know he was safe.

Unable to bear the waiting, she sneaked out to the edge of the arena fence and tried Brook's number again. It rang for ages. In the distance, she could see Livvy and Jester entering the ring.

The crowd gave a cheer – Livvy and Seasonal Jester, the UK favourites. All the while, the sound of Brook's phone rang in her ear. Then she heard a click.

'Tilly?'

'Brook! Oh, thank goodness!'

'Hey, sis! What's up? You sound stressed? Although, I can't really talk now. I'm exercising Solo. We're having a nice, relaxed hack, then he's got the rest of the day off. He worked so hard yesterday . . .'

He paused. She could hear him hushing Solo, as though he was trying to steady him. She could also hear the sound of traffic in the background. They were near a road. Angela always warned riders to keep two hands on the reins at all times, so using a phone while in the saddle was a big no no, especially near traffic. Nonetheless, Tilly felt so desperate, she had to get Brook's attention. She *had* to get him to listen.

'*Please*,' she said. 'This won't take long. Just let me explain. I know you're busy, but I need your help. Fred Webb has managed to get my phone number. And from what he's said, I'm scared he's about to take Magic. Honestly, I need you to get to Silver Shoe as soon as you can.'

She could hear Brook fumbling.

'Hang on, Tilly,' he said. 'I'm just turning. Say the last bit again?'

He was obviously struggling with Solo. Tilly held the line and waited for him to get composed. Ahead of her, she could see Livvy and Jester jumping their way around the course. They were clear over both elements of the double, clean over the large oxer, but Jester spooked violently on the turn before the yellow planks emblazoned with the sponsor's logo, upset by the giant TV screen. The crowd gasped as, using all her skill, Livvy somehow managed to get him to the fence without penalty.

Brook came back on the line. He sounded breathless.

'Sorry, Tilly. Solo's making a fuss. There's suddenly loads of traffic on Cosford Lane. He's getting a bit spooky. I'll call back later, yeah?'

'Okay. Okay. Just promise me you'll get to

Silver Shoe. You will, won't you?'

'Sure. Okay. Woah! HEY!'

Suddenly, there was a dreadful screeching sound, tyres on tarmac, followed by a whinny, then a shout, then screams. Tilly froze.

'Brook?' she asked. '*Brook*! Are you still there? Answer me! What's happening?'

Brook didn't answer. There was more panicked shouting, then a crunch. It sounded like the phone had been dropped.

'BROOK!' Tilly cried again. 'SPEAK TO ME!'

But the line went dead.

Tilly's mouth dropped open. Adrenalin surged through her body. She stared, wide-eyed, as Livvy and Jester came round the corner to clear the final treble. The crowd leapt to their feed and applauded. Livvy and Jester had jumped to glory, but Tilly was in free-fall.

Even as Livvy and Jester approached, Tilly remained motionless. Frozen to the spot. Livvy was all smiles, but Jester immediately sensed Tilly's distress. He started nudging her with his nose. Livvy dismounted.

'What's wrong?' she asked.

Tilly opened her mouth to speak, but the words didn't come. Instead she burst into tears. Livvy pulled her into hug.

'We did it,' she said. 'Don't worry. We did it. Please don't be upset about earlier. I know I moaned at you, but that's just pre-jump jitters. I'm over it.'

Tilly cried harder.

'It's not that though, is it?' asked Livvy, realising it was something serious. 'Tell me. Maybe I can help?'

Once again, Jester pushed his nose under Tilly's chin. She was grateful for his affection. She did her best to calm herself down, then explained the phone call with Brook.

'I don't know what to do,' she said. 'I'm so frightened for him.'

Livvy took her by the shoulders, her expression cool and calm.

'We'll deal with it,' she said.

Without hesitation, she took Tilly's phone and checked Brook's number, trying it again. The line was definitely dead.

'Okay, so we can assume there's been an accident. There will be people already on the scene, especially if you heard voices down the line, but we can call the emergency services from here and alert them. Just in case.'

She took out her own phone and began tapping the keypad. Tilly felt so relieved to have someone taking control of the situation. And for it to be Livvy of all people – one of the bravest, toughest, feistiest riders in the world. Meanwhile, Tilly held on to Jester. She found his presence calming. The way he stood over her, his head on her shoulder, it was as if he was guarding her, shielding her from trouble.

Livvy spoke at length to the emergency services in England. They confirmed that an accident had already been reported and that an ambulance was on its way to the scene. They couldn't say more than that, but it was reassuring to know that help was on its way.

Through the crowds, Tilly caught a glimpse of Chavez. He waved at her, but all she could do was sniff and sob. So, he too, came straight over.

'Tilly, new girl!' he said. 'What's the matter? Why no smile? You always smile.'

Livvy and Tilly explained the disaster. Chavez shook his head.

'Terrible. What can I do to help?'

'Actually, Chavez,' said Livvy, 'I want to take Tilly to the medical tent. I think she's in shock. Could you look after Jester for me, please? He'll be needed for the prize-giving.'

Chavez looked at his watch.

'Ah, Salvatore will be waiting. He has a press conference lined up. He won't be happy if I . . .' He looked at Tilly, thought for a moment, then smiled. 'No problem, Livvy. Salvatore can wait. This is far more important.'

'Thank you so much.'

He took Jester's reins, then gave Tilly's arm a squeeze.

'Don't worry, new girl. Your brother will be

okay. You'll see. Trust Chavez.'

Tilly sniffed and started to cry again. Not just because she was worried about Brook and Solo, but because of the kindness Chavez and Livvy were showing her. Despite their busy lives, they were putting everything aside to help her. In that moment, she realised that team work wasn't just about getting to places on time and winning competitions. It was about being there for each other.

The medics – much more accustomed to treating injured riders – were surprised to find themselves looking after an anxious young groom. They gave Tilly a warm, sugary drink and checked her pulse, then told her to sit quietly, out of the sun and away from the noise. Livvy sat with her, phone at the ready, in case there was any news, but as Tilly recovered she started to feel guilty about taking up Livvy's time.

'I'm sorry,' she whispered. 'This is your chance to enjoy yourself, isn't it? Now that you've done everything you need to do for the competition, you should be out there celebrating, not sitting here with me.'

'To be honest, Tilly, I'm not bothered about the competition right now. I just want to know that you and Brook are okay. I have to ask though, why were you talking to him on the phone when you knew he was in the saddle?'

Tilly looked at her feet, and felt the guilt wash over her.

'I'm worried about Magic,' she said.

'Magic – why?'

'Remember at Junior Squad camp, when Kya was teasing me about Magic not being mine, about him being a rescue horse?'

Livvy nodded.

'Well, there's a man called Fred Webb . . .'

Reluctantly, Tilly explained the whole story about how Fred Webb had started contacting her, and how she'd been ignoring his messages, hoping it would all just go away.

'Oh, Tilly. You should have told Angela, or your parents, or *someone* . . . we could have helped. Horse theft is a massive problem all over the world. And it becomes even more of a problem when a horse starts to do well. As soon as money gets involved, people get greedy. But just because Magic's ownership is uncertain, it doesn't mean this Fred Webb person has the right to start sending you intimidating messages.'

Tilly nodded. She was beginning to realise how silly it was that she and Brook had kept the problem all to themselves.

'For all you know,' Livvy continued, 'the whole thing might be a hoax. And even if Fred Webb *does* have Magic's passport to prove he owned Magic, I'd be rather concerned about his level of care, considering, as you say, you found Magic undernourished and abandoned at a roadside. From what you've told me, you saved Magic's life. Anyone would rather see a horse looked after by someone who cared for them, rather than someone who didn't.'

Suddenly Tilly's phone rang. She jumped to it.

'Hello?'

'Hi, Tilly.'

It was Brook's mum, Mrs Ashton-Smith. She sounded calm, but exhausted.

'I gather you know what's happened. Brook said he was on the phone to you at the time.'

'You've spoken to him?' asked Tilly anxiously. 'Is he okay?'

'He's in hospital. They're getting ready to take him down for surgery, so —'

'*Surgery?*'

Tilly's eyes welled with tears again. Livvy held her other hand.

'It's his pelvis, I'm afraid. It's badly shattered. They're going to operate and put a few pins in.'

Tilly gasped.

'What happened?'

'Apparently, Solo spooked. They were at a gate, near Cosford Lane. A lorry went by and screeched its brakes. Solo's normally okay with traffic but this lorry was big and passed him very close. He really didn't like it. Brook lost control and fell, then Solo fell on top of him.'

'Poor Brook! Is Solo okay?'

'He's being assessed by the vet now. Fingers crossed, but I'm not sure, Tilly. He was very agitated. It took five police officers to get him off the road.'

All because Tilly had been on the phone distracting Brook. Too upset to continue the conversation, she handed the phone to Livvy, who took all the details about what hospital Brook was in and who they could contact for further information.

By the time Livvy was off the phone, Tilly had made up her mind.

'I've got to go home,' she said, knowing there were still a couple of days before the return ferry, including the prize-giving and huge party that she had been looking forward to. But even so . . .

'I've got to go. I've got to be with Brook.'

Livvy nodded.

'I understand,' she said. 'I need to find Chavez

and take Jester off his hands, then I'll ring and get you booked onto the next flight home. Don't worry, Tilly. You'll be with him soon.'

Nine

The earliest flight Livvy was able to get for Tilly was first thing next morning. For Tilly it didn't feel soon enough, but she was grateful anyway.

'Thanks so much,' she whispered. 'Sorry, again.'

'No problem,' Livvy reassured her. 'Are you feeling a bit less shaken now?'

'A bit.'

'The prize-giving ceremony is in five minutes.'

Tilly gasped, shocked that she'd completely forgotten about the competition.

'Oh, yes,' she said. 'Do you think you've come first?'

'Top ten, hopefully. Jester jumped brilliantly, but I don't know what the others did after me. I know those few time faults from the cross country are going to be costly.

Livvy had been so occupied with Tilly that she hadn't followed the last part of the competition. The talk going round was that the New Zealanders had done well, but the young Italian had triumphed. The chief judge came to the microphone and coughed, then began to talk in German, followed by English. He congratulated all the competitors and their teams, then called the winners to the podium in reverse order. Third and second were indeed the New Zealanders and the overall winner was . . .

Tilly closed her eyes and *imagined* the judge was about to say, 'Tilly and Magic Spirit', but of course, the judge gave a small smile and announced:

'Miss Alessandro Biela and her horse, Diavalo!'

Everybody cheered. There were lots of hugs

and kisses and happy chatter. Tilly gazed up at the Italian girl's face and realised she wasn't much older than her, a couple of years or so.

'That'll be you one day,' said a voice behind her. It was Livvy.

Tilly managed a smile.

'I wish,' she said.

They both studied the screen above the podium, which was now showing the rest of the rankings. Fingers crossed.

'Sixth place!' said Tilly, when Livvy's name came up.

'Good enough,' said Livvy. 'It's a decent position, even if it's not a win. I'm really pleased with Jester. He's such a good horse. And at least this year's overall winner is worthy. That Italian girl works ultra-hard.'

Just then, Salvatore Alvarez' name flashed up: but it was at the very bottom.

'Ouch,' said Livvy. 'I guess that'll hurt his pride.'

That evening, after packing her bags and talking at length to her mum and dad about everything, *including* the messy situation with Magic Spirit and Fred Webb, Tilly decided to go down to the stables to say goodbye to Jester. Livvy had relieved her of all grooming duties, but she didn't want to leave without giving him a final hug.

It had been a hot day and the air was still warm. For once, the stable block was peaceful. A few tired horses were resting in their stables. Everyone else was celebrating the end of the competition. As Tilly entered, Jester bobbed his head over the door. He pricked his ears and whickered when he saw her.

'I'm afraid I've come to say goodbye,' said Tilly, sneaking him a mint from her pocket. 'But I just wanted to say how fantastic I think you are and how much I've loved grooming you.'

Jester snorted and gave her an affectionate nudge.

'I'll come and visit you back in England. But

now I have to leave. I have to get back to my brother . . .' She cast her eyes down, pained by her thoughts, ' . . . who is *hopefully* going to be feeling okay after his horrible injury. And then of course there's Solo, poor Solo.'

She held back a tear.

'Please let them be okay,' she whispered.

Instinctively, Jester nuzzled her face. Tilly just hugged him and absorbed the wonderful, soothing warmth of his body.

A few minutes later, Chavez came down the corridor.

'Hey, Tilly, new girl, I thought I'd find you here. You okay?'

Tilly sniffed.

'I will be when I see my brother and our horses.'

'I'll keep my fingers crossed for you all.'

'Thanks.'

'I'm sorry Majesty wasn't placed higher,' said Tilly.

'Ah,' said Chavez, 'maybe it's a good thing. Maybe it will teach Salvatore a lesson.'

'Is Salvatore cross?'

'He's furious. He's shouting at the rest of our team as we speak. But I've walked away. I'm done. Once we get back to Spain, I'm handing in my notice. He can find another groom to shout at.'

Tilly smiled.

'Good for you,' she said. 'But won't you miss Majesty?'

'So much,' he said, then his eyes twinkled. 'But Chavez has a plan.'

'What plan?'

'Ah, Tilly, over the years I've saved lots of money, *all* my money, in fact. Majesty is coming to the end of his eventing career, but I know this royal family, they just give these expensive horses away if they are no use to the prince. To them they are machines, not animals. Majesty can live out his retirement with me. It will be perfection.'

Tilly laughed, delighted for her new friend.

'Fantastic,' she said. 'Can I come and visit?' Shyly, she pulled a bracelet from the pocket of her breeches. 'Look, I made this for you, from Majesty's tail hairs. It's just like the one I always wear. It means that Magic and I are never really apart.'

'Thank you, and I hope you will visit. You'll be welcome any time.'

Ten

Early next morning, Livvy called a taxi for Tilly. She helped her carry her bag down to the yard, gave her a hug and waved her off. As the taxi left the lakes and pine forests behind, Tilly felt a pang of regret that she was leaving Lühmuhlen in such upsetting circumstances. She did her best to focus on getting home, seeing her parents, hugging Magic and visiting Brook.

The taxi driver dropped her outside the airport and helped her find a trolley for her bags. She hadn't flown on her own before and felt a little nervous, but everyone was very helpful and kind. Once inside the departure lounge, she bought a magazine and a coke, and then stared at the planes landing and taking off. She twiddled her horsehair bracelets. She checked her phone, dreading the prospect of more missed calls from Fred Webb. Thankfully, there was just a string of text messages from all her friends, expressing their shock about Brook's accident.

One from Anna: *Jst hrd news. OMG! Hope everything okay. Call as soon as you're home. Anna xx*

One from Ben: *Total nightmare. So gutted for them both. But they'll pull through – they're strong. Luv u, Ben xx*

One from Harry: *Tilly, U ok? Call if you need anything. Thinking of u. xx*

And even one from Kya. There wasn't much to it, but at least she'd made the effort: *oxo kya oxo*

The flight was short. Even though Tilly had her regrets about leaving Lühmuhlen, when she finally took a step on English tarmac, a huge sense of relief washed over her. As soon as she got through passport control and customs, she saw her parents waiting. She ran towards them.

'Don't worry, Tiger Lil',' said her dad, hugging her to his chest. 'Don't you worry. Everything's going to be fine.'

They went straight to the car. Usually after Tilly had done something exciting like a competition or a training session, they spent the whole journey home talking about nothing else. This time, the discussion was all about Brook and Solo. Lühmuhlen was hardly mentioned.

'He's had an operation,' Tilly's mum explained. 'The surgeon is pleased with the way it's gone. I think they had to put three pins in his hip though.'

Tilly winced. There was only one question on her mind.

'So, when will he be able to ride again?'

Tilly's mum went quiet.

'One thing at a time, eh, Tilly? He's got to recover first. He might be in hospital for weeks yet. Then he'll need physio. And he might need some help to walk initially. We'll see about riding.'

Tilly nodded solemnly. 'And what about Solo? What's the news?'

'Not so good, I'm afraid. One of his front legs is injured. He's still under sedation. Hopefully he'll be okay, but only time will tell.'

Tilly sniffed. She knew what happened to horses with leg problems. A bad leg could end a career and if it was serious enough, it could end a life. She clenched her fists, took a deep breath. She had to be strong. She knew she had to be strong for her brother.

'Let's go and see Brook, shall we?' said her mum, chivvying her along. 'He's ready for visitors.'

Realising that Tilly and Brook would need some time alone, Mr and Mrs Redbrow waited in the hospital café. A nurse led Tilly through the hospital corridor to Brook's ward. The curtains were drawn around his cubicle, but Tilly could hear the sound of televised horse-racing from inside. That made her smile. Even in a hospital bed, Brook couldn't bear to be far from horses. The nurse pulled back the curtain.

'Tilly!'

'Hi, bro!'

Brook switched off the TV.

'I'm so glad you're here,' he said. 'You poor thing. You must have been terrified. They told me you heard it all down the phone . . .'

Tilly took his hand and squeezed it.

'Don't worry about *me*,' she said. 'It's you who matters. Oh Brook, I'm so, so sorry.'

She glanced down the bed, to the metal frame that was caging his hips.

Seeing her worried face, Brook explained, 'It's just so I don't move while the bone heals.'

'Is it painful?'

'I'm full of painkillers, Tilly. I honestly wouldn't know. I tell you what though, if I'm *seriously* going to have to lie still for two weeks, I'm going to get SO bored. You'd better visit every day.'

'You know I will.'

'So, how was Lühmuhlen?'

Tilly couldn't believe that after everything Brook had been through, he was still asking about her. Typical Brook, always thinking of other people.

'It was good,' she said.

'Just good?'

'Just good.'

'And have you seen Magic, yet?'

'No. I came straight here.'

'Wow! I'm honoured,' said Brook. 'But you should go and see Magic. I know how worried you've been.'

This time, Brook squeezed *her* hand.

'I will,' she said, amazed by her brother's generosity. 'And Solo, too. I mean, while you're stuck in here, do you want me to go and see him for you?'

Brook looked away. He turned his face to the

window and just stared out, too upset to talk. Tilly felt crushed with sorrow for him, knowing there was nothing she could do to change what had happened.

'By the way, I got loads of text messages asking about you,' she said, as brightly as she could. 'Even Kya sent some hugs and kisses.'

Brook snapped out of his gloom and groaned.

'Don't be fooled,' he said. 'Do you know she's been going around telling people what a show-off you are, with all your Lühmuhlen selfies?'

Tilly just rolled her eyes and laughed. A week ago, news like this would have upset her. Now, it seemed trivial.

'She's pathetic,' she said. Brook agreed.

Tilly left Brook's bedside feeling better. His braveness was reassuring. Even so, as she wandered back along the hospital corridor to find her parents, she knew that the look in his eyes when she'd asked him about Solo would haunt her forever. Behind all the jokes and smiles and medication, she'd seen a look of such sadness, such loss. It was heartbreaking. And even if Solo made a complete recovery, their chances of winning the Junior Championships were ruined now. In fact, Tilly realised, it was possible their entire eventing careers were over – before they'd properly begun. It was so unfair.

Knowing that Magic would be next on her agenda, Tilly's parents drove her straight to Silver Shoe. Before her dad even turned the car engine off, Tilly leapt out and ran up the yard. To her surprise, the first person she saw was Harry Grey.

'Huh? What are you doing here?' she said.

'Waiting for you.'

'Oh.'

'Angela called me. She said you were coming back. I wanted to check you're okay. Thought you might need a friend.'

Tilly smiled, flattered and a little surprised. 'Thanks.'

'I know it's not a good time, Tilly, but . . . we

said we'd go hacking. It might take your mind off things. I mean, if you fancy it?'

'Well, I need to exercise Magic and . . . yes . . . I'd like to,' she said.

The sight of Magic in the field was blissful. Tilly called him, saddle and bridle in hand. When he noticed her, he tossed his head, bucked joyfully, shuddered all over and cantered towards her. Tilly threw her arms around his neck.

'Oh, boy,' she said. 'Have *I* missed *you*!'

Magic nuzzled her shoulder and sniffed her face.

'Fancy a ride?'

Immediately, he dipped his head, so that she could place his bridle over his ears. His grace and affection felt like a moment of pure joy among all the bad stuff. There was so much uncertainty, so much change to get used to, but Magic was still here and he was *hers* – for now, at least. As she placed the saddle on his back, she thought of how much she wanted to compete, how much she wanted to make it to the very top of the sport. Like Livvy, she wanted to succeed. And now she wouldn't just be doing it for herself, but for Brook and Solo too. With a deep breath and prayer for courage, she put her foot into the stirrup, swung into the saddle, then walked up the path to where Harry and Hunter were waiting in the yard.

'We'll do it for them, Magic,' she whispered. 'For them.'

Pippa Funnell

"Winning is amazing for a minute, but then I am striving again to reach my next goal."

I began learning to ride when I was six, on a little pony called Pepsi.

When I was seven, I joined my local Pony Club – the perfect place to learn more about riding and caring for horses.

By the time I was fourteen and riding my first horse, Sir Barnaby, my dream of being an event rider was starting to take shape.

Two years later, I was offered the opportunity to train as a working pupil in Norfolk with Ruth McMullen, the legendary riding teacher. I jumped at the chance.

In 1987, Sir Barnaby and I won the individual gold together at the Young Rider European Championships, which was held in Poland.

Since then, hard work and determination have taken me all the way to the biggest eventing competitions in the world. I've been lucky and had success at major events like Bramham, Burghley, Badminton, Luhmühlen, Le Lion d'Angers, Hickstead, Blenheim, Windsor, Saumur, Pau, Kentucky – and the list goes on . . .

I married William Funnell in 1993. William is an international show jumper and horse breeder. He has helped me enormously with my show jumping. We live on a farm in the beautiful Surrey countryside – with lots of stables!

Every sportsman or woman's wildest dream is to be asked to represent their country at the Olympics. So in 2000, when I was chosen for the Sydney Olympics, I was delighted. It was even more special to be part of the silver medal winning team.

Then, in 2003, I became the first (and only) person to win eventing's most coveted prize – the Rolex Grand Slam. The Grand Slam (winning three of the big events in a row – Badminton, Kentucky and Burghley) is the only three-day eventing slam in the sporting world.

2004 saw another Olympics and another call-up. Team GB performed brilliantly again and won another well-deserved silver medal, and I was lucky enough to win an individual bronze.

Having had several years without any top horses, I spent my time producing youngsters, so it was great in 2010 when one of those came through – Redesigned, a handsome chestnut gelding. In June that year I won my third

Bramham International Horse Trials title on Redesigned. We even managed a clear show jumping round in the pouring rain! By the end of 2010, Redesigned was on the squad for the World Championships in Kentucky where we finished fifth.

Today, as well as a hectic competition schedule, I'm also busy training horses for the future. At the Billy Stud, I work with my husband, William, and top breeder, Donal Barnwell, to produce top-class sport horses.

And in between all that I love writing the *Tilly's Pony Tails* books, and I'm also a trustee of World Horse Welfare, a fantastic charity dedicated to giving abused and neglected horses a second chance in life. For more information, visit their website at www.worldhorsewelfare.org.